EZRA AND NOVA'S BAYOU

Preface

Ezra and Nova lived in the Bayous of Louisiana. They led amazingly simple lives. They had two children Jennifer and Buck. The family may have come from a poor environment, but they grew strong and became rich. They never forgot where they came from. They always helped others. While writing this book I never want Jennifer and Buck forgotten. One thing for sure, the family will never forget them.

Down in the bayou where the green grass grows, cypress trees, muddy water, and swamps all around, lived a man that I will call Ezra. Ezra and his wife Nova lived a simple life in the bayous of Louisiana. He lived amongst alligators, snakes, wild animals, and numerous poisonous insects. You had to have a boat to get to his home or you could use a very narrow dirt road which was muddy most of the time. In addition to the mud, the weather was always extremely hot and humid.

Ezra lived in the bayous of Louisiana all his 29 years with his mother and father. He was an only child so we know that he must have been lonely most of the time. The family home was so isolated that no one would come and visit.

Ezra was a fisherman, and his mother was a housewife who made beautiful quilts and sold them in the marketplace in New Orleans.

Ezra loved animals and put you in the mind of a Tarzan. In the forest he knew all of the animals that lived there. He also knew all the poisonous and non-poisonous plants. He knew which ones he could use as medicine. They didn't have much money, so they had to doctor themselves a lot. Living this lifestyle was a hard life, but it made him tough as alligator skin.

Ezra had some family that lived in New Orleans but didn't get to visit them often. His family didn't visit them because of all the swamp and mud where they lived. Sometimes Ezra and Nova needed help from their family, but they never asked them. One time Ezra's father fell and broke his hip and was laid up for about a year. It was up to Nova and Ezra to help his parents along with a few welfare checks to help them through the tough times. Ezra had to fish for shrimp and go hunting to put food on the table just to survive. At this time in his life, he was a very strong young man.

His dad finally was well enough to go back to work and could take care of his mother. It was a blessing because the welfare checks were just about ready to run out. God came in right on time to rescue them. When you live in a desolate place you learn to work as hard as you can. You go to church and trust God.

While growing up Ezra had a dog named Smokey. They were best friends and went everywhere together. Ezra had to teach Smokey about the wild animals and alligators to never go around them. Smokey was a very smart dog. One time Ezra was walking along one of the swampy paths and Smokey killed a poisonous snake and saved his life. He was forever grateful to Smokey.

By this time, Ezra wanted to venture out to see some of the world. To him, a small town would be an advantage to him, so his dad bought him a Jeep. It was an older one and he learned to drive it on all of the muddy and narrow roads where he lived. He finally learned to drive well enough to go to town by himself. He decided to drive to New Orleans one cloudy Saturday afternoon. He wanted to see the marketplace and some of the art that was there. His mother went to the market for years selling things that she had made. There were so many people there and the market tables were full of several types of wares. To Ezra it was a site to see. There were people playing music on the street everywhere. There were people who had painted their bodies looking like clowns. He decides to buy himself a necklace and get something to eat.

This is where he met the love of his life. She was standing in front of one of the fruit tables. All of a sudden, she accidentally knocked over a box of oranges that fell to the ground. She looked so hurt that he felt sorry for her and began helping her pick the oranges up and put them back in the box. As he was helping her their eyes met. She had the most beautiful dark eyes he had ever seen. When Ezra got back home, he couldn't get those beautiful eyes out of his mind. Some say if you look into the eyes of a person, you can almost feel who they are. Ezra believed this was true.

Ezra could not get those beautiful eyes out of his mind so the next weekend he drove to New Orleans. He went to the same restaurant and as he began to order his meal he looked over and saw the beautiful lady that he had been thinking of ever since the last weekend. He decided that he must know her name, so he walked over to her table, acting as if he had just run into her again. Ezra said "Oh, we meet again. May I join you?" She hesitated at first, but then she said yes. They had dinner and talked. He asked her name. She said it was Amanda. He thought it was a strange name. He had never heard that name before. She said it meant Gift from God, as a blessed child. They talked for a couple of hours. It was starting to get late, and Ezra had to get home before it got dark. Driving in bayou country at night on all those back roads wasn't a good thing to do. She thanked him for the meal, then Ezra went on his way home. She thought he was so handsome and polite.

One month later, she ran into him again in town. This time she asked him if he would like to go to the art festival. He said he would love to go. They went to the festival and admired all of the art that was displayed. Some art was beautiful, some they couldn't figure out what it was. It was definitely an experience for Ezra. He didn't want her to know that he had never been to an event like this before. After the date he asked Amanda if they could start dating. She said ye right away. There was something about Ezra she knew she could really love and trust. She had just turned 21 years old. She thought to herself, what would she have to lose. This could turn into something beautiful. This could be the love of her life. He was so handsome. His eyes really reached out to her. Her heart skipped a beat whenever she saw him.

After a few months of dating, Ezra asked Amanda if they could become engaged. She said yes. They were incredibly happy and deeply in love.

In the meantime, Ezra knew he would have to show her where he lived in the bayou. They decided on a Saturday afternoon. It would take them 2 hours to get there. It was time to show her where he lived, how he lived, and to meet his family. At first Amanda enjoyed the ride in the back country even though the ride was bumpy and muddy. The further they went the darker it got. She saw all the cypress trees hanging over the road. No wonder they didn't get much sundown here. It was 2 o'clock and it was dark already. When they got to the house her heart sank. She took one look and said to herself that she didn't like this. The house looked like a shack that hadn't been lived in for years. Ezra took one look at her and knew she didn't like it. She wondered how anyone could live like this. Amanda wasn't used to anything like this. She was used to the good things in life. After all, her father was a doctor. To most people she lived like a queen.

She really didn't want to get out of the car. Ezra opened the car door and there was his father Ezra I and his mother Nova welcoming her to their home. Unbelievably the house was nice looking on the inside. Ezra's mother had beautiful things hanging on the walls. She had beautiful chairs and couches. The house really had a spark of coziness. His parents were really nice, and she could see where he got his good upbringing from. His mother cooked a wonderful meal that was unbelievably delicious. His mother's table was set eloquently with fine china and linen napkins. It was a very festive dinner. Amanda enjoyed their company very much. Coming from where she did, they made her feel at home and comfortable.

A lot of people never go out to the bayou because of all the danger and difficulty. It took an incredibly special kind of person to live there. It could be a very hazardous place to live.

It was getting dark, and it was time for Amanda to return home. She was ready to get out of the bayou. There were many dangerous animals, and some criminals were known to live out there also. On her way home she could not figure out how anyone could live there. Many people did not have running water or inside bathrooms.

During the following year, Ezra worked hard to make repairs to his home with Nova, his wife of many years. During that time his father passed away. That was a terrible time for Ezra, his only son. His father raised him up to be the man that he was. A real man. His father was a strong man. He always fought for what was right. Never trying to beat anyone out of anything. He was truly an anchor for his family. Ezra didn't know how he was going to get along without him.

This is when Amanda stepped in. Their relationship grew and they were deeply in love. At first, she couldn't understand why Ezra wanted to continue to fix the old place up. He was fixing it up so Amanda would feel safe and comfortable there. So, in the spring of that year, he asked her to marry him and of course she said yes.

Her side of the family wanted her to have a big wedding with many guests to celebrate their life together. Amanda didn't think Ezra would like that so well, thinking he would like a smaller ceremony, but Ezra knew what he was going to do. And that was pleasing Amanda. That was going to be his life's work. He hated suits and dress shoes and all the fancy things that were going on at the wedding, but he knew it was for only one day, so he could do it. Their wedding was going to be at the church her family was a member of. It was a noticeably big church. The church would be full of people he did not know, but if Amanda was happy that was all that mattered.

Her family was nice to him, but sometimes he felt he didn't fit in. He knew he was also marrying the family. Some way, somehow, he felt they could all make it together.

The wedding was beautiful, and Amanda looked like a queen. Ezra asked one of his friends to be his best man. Some of his family attended. Of course, his mother was there. It was a wedding of a lifetime. At the reception, Ezra drank a little too much wine and got tipsy. That was ok because they had a limousine to drive them home. The limousine was white, and can you imagine it driving though the bayou? First of all, it was built low. Ezra was afraid the muffler would fall off because of all the mud and the big potholes. They made it home safely and Ezra was really relieved.

When they got to the house it looked rather good. Ezra had painted the house inside and out. Amanda realized that it wasn't so bad after all. It was paid for and was going to be her home.

Nova, Ezra's mom, gifted them a honeymoon in the Florida Keys for 3 days. That's all she could afford. Ezra had never been out of the swamps for more than a day, so he was really excited to go. He had never flown on a plane. It seemed a little scary to him. Amanda was used to flying. Her family had taken many vacations that required air travel. During the flight Amanda held Ezra's hand to let him know that he didn't have to be afraid with her. She knew that together they could conquer anything. They felt that they could be a safe rock for each other.

When they took off, he really felt funny, like he wanted to throw up. There were so many people on the plane, adults and children. Ezra was so glad it was a straight shot to the keys with no layovers. When they were beginning to land, Ezra was looking over the ocean. He thought it was a beautiful sight. Something he had never seen before. He loved it, even though it was a little scary. When they landed, they took a shuttle to the hotel, and boy was it hot. Hotter than the bayou.

They went to explore the area and there were a lot of open-air markets like in New Orleans. Many people spoke Spanish. Ezra and Amanda needed an interpreter at times. Of course, many people in the restaurants and markets spoke English.

The Keys reminded Him of the Bayou a little. There was so much water around and many colorful things to see. One thing that got him was all the chickens running around all over the place. And the roosters crowing at the crack of dawn. He said something sort of funny to him. He saw this island in the middle of the ocean. There were no highways to get there. The only way to get there was by boat or plane. The houses were big and beautiful. He knew who ever lived there was very wealthy. It was almost like his home, but his family wasn't wealthy. He thought that it was nice to be able to live like that and not have to worry about where the money was coming from. He thought that one day he wanted to live just like that. Deep down in his heart he really wanted something like that for Amanda, his mother, and himself. The job that he had at this time made that impossible.

After 3 days the honeymoon was over, and it was time to head home. Ezra was doing a lot of thinking on the way back home. He wanted to live just like that. He knew it would make Amanda and his mom incredibly happy. At this time, that's all he wanted to do. Ezra knew now that there were better places to live. The trip really opened his eyes. He thought that was what his mother was trying to show him with the trip. He knew he couldn't change things right away, but he knew a change was coming one day.

As time passed Ezra could sense that Amanda wasn't happy living in the bayou. She didn't come right out and say it, but he knew her like a book and could feel her feelings. After living there for 6 months he decided to move into town. He told Amanda and could instantly see the twinkle in her eyes. She was so happy. It was too isolated where they lived. Sometimes really scary at night. She had her job and so did he. It would be better for both of them and their jobs. Ezra thought that even if he moved, he could still come back to the bayou occasionally. It had been his home up until now and he would always find his way back. He had learned many things living in the bayou. It taught you how to survive without anything. It seemed to Ezra that everything in town was easy for people. At first, it was hard for Ezra to live in the city. All the traffic, buildings being so close together, and all of the hustle and bustle of people going here and there. But because Amanda liked it there, he made himself as comfortable as possible. They were able to save money and Amanda's parents helped. Amanda was a bargain hunter and a saver even though she came from a wealthy family. They lived in a two-bedroom apartment overlooking Bourbon Street. There was always something going on there. There were funerals in New Orleans where the family and community would march behind the hearse. Live bands would be playing, and everyone was dancing. They really celebrated the deceased homegoing sometimes playing When the Saints Go Marching In. Another thing about New Orleans is that they couldn't bury them underground because they say the ground has too much sand in it. If they did so they say that the graves would fill up with water when it rains. Most people were buried in crypts above ground.

Ezra continued to work at the fish factory. He had been there a few years. He liked it there and liked the people he worked with. He still kept his house in the bayou. Every once in a while, he would wander back just to check on his home. One evening he decided to go back home and check on the house. Once he got there, he noticed that lights were on inside. He thought that someone must be inside, so he went and walked up on the porch and opened the front door. When he opens the door there are two young women staring him in the face that look to be bruised and battered all over their bodies. They looked to be of Creole descent and had very dark eyes. They were as startled as he was. Ezra asked them how long they had been living there. They told him several weeks. They went on to tell him that a man had kidnapped them and made them prostitute for him. Luckily, the man had gone somewhere and was not there at the time. He looked around his house that he had worked so hard on, and it was all messed up. Trash was everywhere. He was really mad, not at the women, but at the man for not only tearing his house up, but for also mistreating these women. He told them to gather their things up and to leave. They told him they had nowhere to go. Ezra told them to get into his car and that he would get them out of there. They were hesitant to leave because they said the man would find them and kill them. He also told them that if they tried to run away from the house that they would be eaten by one of the many wild animals that lived in the bayou. Ezra told them he would take them to the police station. They were so afraid. Ezra told them that they could not stay in this house any longer. He took them to town. That was the end of it as far as he knew. As far as the girls were concerned. He still had a problem. The man was still living in his house. He thought that maybe he might come after him because he took his girls. This was a real problem for Ezra. He knew this could get messy. Living in the bayou, anything could happen, and no one would know what happened to you. He could be dumped in the swamp and eaten by alligators. The police would treat it like another missing persons report. Ezra knew this happened many times when he was growing up.

What he feared most started happening. The man began calling his house in town, scaring Amanda with threats. Ezra did not know that this man was a member of one of the drug cartels of Louisiana. When he found out who he was he knew they were in trouble. The man not only was involved in prostitution but was running a meth lab in his home. Amanda was really frightened. Not only was she the daughter of a doctor, but her family was also well known in the city. Ezra knew it would be quite easy for the man to find them, so he sent her to Nashville for a while. He had a friend who lived there who was a famous football player named Roger.

At first, Amanda did not want to go, but she was afraid not to. She got away just in time because about three hours later the man sent someone to blow up their apartment. Now Ezra was out of a place to live. He couldn't go back to the house in the bayou and his apartment was just blown up. He couldn't ask his in-laws for a place to live because he would put them in danger. Ezra knew what to do with people like that. He hadn't been raised in the bayou for nothing. His father was a sharpshooter and had taught Ezra to protect himself. He knew if he went back there, he would have a chance to survive. So, Ezra went back home to the bayou.

He knew how to set traps for anything that came near the house. If anyone came up the road near his house, he had traps set for them. There was a small bridge a half mile from his house. He set bombs all around it. He did not care if it blew up, he had other ways to get out of the bayou. He had big guns and plenty of ammo. If this man thought he could come into his territory without any trouble, then he was wrong. Ezra waited to ambush him for three days. He knew when he came back, he wouldn't be by himself, so Ezra called a few friends to come and help him. Ezra was surrounded by an occasional alligator and poisonous snakes, but he was not afraid. When Ezra was small, he remembered that some men were not supposed to be near the house. Ezra's dad got rid of them really quick. He caught some poisonous snakes and put them along the road. Some snakes even fell out of the trees. Those people left right away. His dad said that you must get them before they get you.

He finally saw them coming and set off the bombs. For some reason, only two went off. They missed the bridge all together and didn't kill them all. Ezra could see what was going on because he had cameras up all around his house. He put tire spikes on the road to blow their tires. He also set traps inside of the house in case they made it in. The cartel did eventually get close to the house and started shooting the house up. Ezra and his friends decided it was time to get out of there. There was a secret underground tunnel that went from the basement to a safe way from the house. Just as they emerged from the tunnel the house blew up. Come to find out, the guy who was after them had just entered the house as it blew up. It was sad for Ezra because this was his family home. The house that he grew up in. His mom and dad didn't have much but at least it was home.

He called Amanda and his mother Nova and told them they could come home. He told them everything is alright. Amanda was happy to be back home.

They had to start all over again and find a new place to live. Amanda went to stay with her family and Nova and Ezra went to stay with some of their relatives for a while. Finally, he found a nice small home for them to live in.

Ezra was an only child and lately had started thinking about having a family of his own someday. He started wanting to build another home in the bayou so his children could have the experience of living there. He was not ashamed of his childhood. Everyone's childhood is not the same. This world would be a heck of a world if it was. Ezra couldn't wait to start life all over again. The last month was hell.

Ezra liked working at the fish factory. He liked the people he worked with. They would give each other nicknames. He worked there for a lot of years. They would go out on Friday nights and play cards at the corner bar. They were a nice group of guys. They were hardworking and just down to earth. One night one of the guys had a winning streak and won most of the money. He was leaving the bar walking to his car when another guy who had been in the bar saw him leave. He knew that he had just won some money.

He follows him and knocks him out and robs him. He took about 300 dollars. When the other guys came out to leave, they saw him knocked out on the ground by his car. They took him to the hospital and after a few hours he was released. He was ok. No serious injuries. Of all the times they had gone out, nothing like this had ever happened. It had to be an outsider. They decided that they would find this guy and give him a good whipping. When they get done with him, he will never rob anyone else. One of the guys thought he had seen someone he had not recognized. They saw him getting out of his car that night. They were sure that he didn't live around there. Come to find out he was a relative of one of the guys that worked at the factory. He was downtown at the market when one of the guys saw him. They decided not to beat him up because of all the people around. So, they took him to the bayou and put him in a shack for a night. He was in his early twenties. They had to tie him up, put him in the car, and take him there. He was crying all the way. They put him in the old shack, tied his hands behind his back. There were no windows, and it was dark as a dungeon. They wanted to teach him a lesson. They wanted him to think twice before he did that again. Ezra said this is what we do to people that do us wrong. He had no food or any water. They left him there all night and came back the next day. Luckily, they did because there were coyotes circling the shack getting ready to attack him. Luckily, they got there when they did because they could be charged with kidnapping and maybe murder if the coyotes got a hold of him. The man was out of his mind when they went back and got him. The guys that took him there were just as happy as the man was that he was okay. That's how things can go wrong sometimes. The man said he would pay back the 300 dollars and would never do anything like that again. After that, sometimes they would see him in the streets and just smile at each other and go about their business.

Amanda never knew the kind of life Ezra had growing up. She had always lived in New Orleans where everything was modern and free spirited.

Now it was the time of year when people could hunt alligators for money. Ezra always went out with his father. His father made a lot of money during this time which carried his family through the rest of the year. There was a man in the bayou who owned a bait shop. You could also rent boats to go out on. The owner's name was Lewis, and they went there every season. Lewis knew most of the people in the area and had sold them bait or rented them a boat. Lewis always expected to see them during this time.

Well, it was a beautiful morning, waking up to the beautiful sunrise. Not a cloud in the sky. It was a day that you were happy to be alive. Everything was going well for Ezra and Amanda. They both were working steady and saving all the money they could, getting ready for a wonderful week. They were incredibly happy. Ezra mentioned to Amanda that it might be a suitable time to start thinking about having children. Amanda didn't think it was a good idea at first because she wanted to wait until they got into their own home. Amanda always wanted to plan things ahead of time. She also knew that things didn't always go as planned.

Most of the time, New Orleans was a beautiful place to live except during the occasional hurricane. They wanted to have a house away from the ocean, maybe on a hill. Amanda knew these houses would be in the hundreds of thousands of dollars. Amanda's family could help them get the home of their dreams. But Ezra said, "no way". Ezra's parents never asked anyone for anything. They lived in the bayou and didn't need much to live there. Ezra would be content to live in a very modest home. He wanted to live close to the earth, never having his head in the clouds. Many times, on his way to work, he would see homeless people underneath the bridges, living on the streets. They were also along the road, some sleeping on benches. Once in a while you could see the police come and make them move to somewhere else. Some were so dirty, had rugged clothes, and had holes in their shoes. This made him incredibly sad. He always wondered why some people had to live this way. He and Amanda had talked about one day they could help them, but right now it was just a dream. They wondered why the US government couldn't help more. Many of the homeless could be eligible for disability checks.

Amanda decided she was ready to have a child. She got along fine the first few months. They were getting the baby's room ready, going to the doctor for checkups, and working every day. The time was really going fast. Amanda often walked in the beautiful parks near where she lived. She would watch the young mothers walking with their babies.

One morning, on her way to work, Amanda was getting gas. She happened to look over and saw a young lady with a small child. Five minutes later she saw the young lady leaving the gas station without the child. She thought that was a bit strange. Amanda could see the child running around in the gas station crying. Amanda immediately went over and took the child's hand. The child was crying so hard that she was almost having a fit. Amanda thought the mother might come back but she never did. The owner of the gas station called the police. They came and took the child. They eventually found the young lady. She told them that she was homeless and couldn't take care of her child anymore. They took her to jail and released her the next day. She went on her way, but her child was put in foster care. Amanda thought to herself that it must happen a lot. In the meantime, Amanda was just about ready to have her baby. She told herself that that would never happen to her child.

One early morning when it was raining dogs and cats, she went into labor. She labored for 27 hours. The baby finally came and weighed 8 lbs. And 2 oz. There was something wrong with the baby's heart. It was too small. The doctor said to give it time and it would grow with the body. That was so scary. When they first brought the baby home, they had to bring oxygen with them. The baby had a special nurse and the grandmothers helped out. After a few weeks the baby was doing well enough that she didn't need oxygen anymore. She was breathing normally. By the way, they named her Jennifer. She was a beautiful baby girl. She started smiling right away. Her eyes beamed like bright lights, as if all the time she was trying to tell them that she was going to be alright. As she grew older, her heart grew with her. Jennifer was doing very well. She was slow at doing some things, but Amanda got help and she soon caught up. When she started kindergarten, she was right on track with the other children. It seemed that everything was going well for her at this time.

Jennifer had a great life. Amanda made sure she had lots of friends and lots to do. When she was nine years old, she entered a modeling school for young girls. She was exceptionally talented and could sing and dance. Amanda and Ezra were really proud of her. At this time, they were thinking about having another child. They didn't want Jennifer to grow up being an only child. Amanda got pregnant right away. She carried the baby very well. In the fall of the year their son was born. He was very small but doing well. Of course, Ezra was so happy. They thought their lives were complete. I forgot to say that he was only 3 pounds when he was born.

From the beginning they knew he was a fighter. He kept on growing and knew that he would survive. They loved him so much. That gave him the will to live.

Getting back to Jennifer, by the time she was in the sixth grade, she was a really good model for someone her age. Amanda dressed her lavishly all the time. She made sure her hair was done with ribbons and barrettes every day. It was quite an expense for them. Nova, her grandmother, was immensely proud of her. She helped with some of the expenses some of the time. At age 10, they entered her into a modeling contest, and she came in 1st place. She received a trophy and won 500 dollars. She was a beautiful girl with or without makeup.

Her skin was medium brown, and she had long black curly hair and dark eyes. As time went by, she became a star. In high school she was doing really well in her craft. At the age of 16 her dad bought her a car. She learned to drive quickly. She was extremely popular with the boys and girls at her school.

Her school was on the outskirts of town, so she drove herself to school every day. She graduated with honors and wanted to go to college in New York. Ezra and Amanda had to think long and hard about this because it was so far away. Since Jennifer could model, she could do that and go to school also. That way she could pay her way through college. One of her classmates was going to go to school in New York also. Her parents finally gave their consent for her to go to New York to study and model.

In the fall of the year, off she went to the big city. She caught a train from New Orleans to New York. On her way there, she saw a lot of the country. Places she had never seen before. The train ride was a wonderful experience for her. Jennifer and her classmate Madyson arrived at the same time at the train station in NYC. She had never seen so many people in one place in all her life. Someone from the school came to meet them at the station. They were grateful that someone came to meet them. The buildings were so tall. The lights were so bright. It was the middle of the day. People were walking all over the place. She thought New Orleans was bright, but this was another type of brightness. It wasn't like the sun coming up in New Orleans. It was really a little scary but beautiful.

The representative from the school took them directly to the school. It was big. She thought that she would like it there. She had never been so far away from home before, and her friend hadn't either. This modeling school was supposed to be in the United States. Ezra and Amanda were a little worried at first about her being so far away. Jennifer had a good head on her shoulders even though she had been sheltered.

The first year she did very well. She learned how to put together a wardrobe, walk the runway, and how to apply makeup. Madyson was also doing well. While in school they were permitted to do modeling jobs, which allowed them to make money. You could say that they both were doing well., but there were men who wanted to take advantage of them. One day they got a call from someone wanting them to model for the company near Queens. The pay would be good, so they decided to do the job. They didn't know it was going to be in an apartment building in the bad part of town. They arrived at about 9:00 pm ready to model. When they got there, there were too many men there. It really didn't seem right to Jennifer. Madyson thought that things didn't seem right also. Immediately they wanted the girls to take of all their clothes. They immediately called the dean at the school and told him what was happening and what was going on. In no time there was a pounding at the door coming to get the girls. The men in the apartment were scared and tried to run. They were so glad that they came and rescued them. That day they learned a valuable lesson. They wouldn't take any more jobs without telling the dorm assistant. New York wasn't New Orleans where they were sheltered.

Jennifer had one more year of school to finish. She continued to model for places like Macy's. She modeled for a lot of the upscale department stores.

The school year was almost over when she decided that she wanted to go to Paris. She heard there were a lot of rich and famous people there. She knew she could make a good amount of money. When Jennifer got to Paris, she didn't have money. She rented a one room flat uptown. Paris was just as beautiful as she thought it would be. The parks and rivers were beautiful. There were many bridges. There was a gold skyscraper in the middle of the city. It would light up day and night. She was lonely at first. She only knew her boss and coworkers.

Jennifer loved beautiful things and beautiful people. She just knew she would fit in with the beautiful people. She was schooled among the best.

Milan Modeling Agency was the best. Elite was another. They had models that graced the covers of Vogue magazine. Ford Modeling is still one of the best in Paris. Visa Modeling is another famous one. Jennifer first went to Vogue modeling. They liked her and wanted her to try out. A week later they called her and offered her a job. They wanted her to model some attire from New Orleans. This would be a piece of cake for her. The first shoot was in front of a beautiful flower garden. She wore beautiful clothes and wore a hat to match. The outfit was brightly colored. The next shoot was on some of the beautiful bridges. Jennifer felt particularly good about how the shoot went. The next month she was on the cover of Vogue magazine. She was delighted and so was her family. Her picture was international. She had become famous. And she was making a lot of money. She moved out of her small apartment. She was not only beautiful. She was smart also. Her friend Madyson was doing quite well in New York. Jennifer wanted her to come to Paris to visit. Madyson said that maybe for the holidays she could because she has time off. The holidays came and Madyson was able to stay a week with her. Jennifer showed her all the beautiful sights and restaurants. They went to see the Eiffel Tower. They had a wonderful time. Jennifer wanted Madyson to stay a little longer. She liked Paris but she liked New York more. She was doing really well there.

Jennifer always kept in touch with her parents and her brother Buck. Back home everything was the same except for Buck growing up and going to college. He wanted to be a lawyer. He was very smart. Even if he was only 3 pounds when he was born, he grew up to be very handsome and healthy. He wanted to be a lawyer for people who were treated unfairly for their crimes. Buck knew that by his father living in the bayou that a lot of those people were not getting the justice that they deserved. He attended Princeton for four years. He studied under some of the greatest professors. Because of all the terrible things going on these days, he couldn't wait to get in the courtroom and to express himself. He defended a lot of people who were innocent. Some were freed, some were not. He just tried his best. Being a lawyer was a remarkable thing but sometimes it could be very frustrating. Buck decided he wanted to go to San Francisco to live and practice law. It was warm there just like in New Orleans.

New Orleans had hurricanes, but California had earthquakes. He could feel the ground shaking under his feet sometimes but nothing big. He knew of some talk of a big earthquake which could destroy San Francisco. He didn't like that or the fact that it was very hilly. He lived in a small apartment overlooking the Golden Gate Bridge. It was very pretty at night. There were all types of people living in San Francisco. You could call them all a bunch of assorted flavors. Most of the people stayed to themselves. You could hear the trolley cars all through the night. It was like people never stopped moving.

Buck went looking for an office for himself. He didn't want to be all the way downtown. It was expensive to have an office there. He had money but he had to be careful with it. He found a small but efficient office space which was big enough for him.

His first case was a young 17-year-old boy. His parents came into his office. The boy was accused of raping a young girl at his school. The boy said he did not do it. Buck took one look at the boy and thought to himself that he was innocent. Come to find out there were a few of the rich kids there that night. The 17-year-old boy was the only black kid there. The rich kid told her to blame it on the black boy. He was poor and couldn't defend himself in court. They took the girl to the hospital and did a rape kit on her. When the DNA evidence came back it proved that the boy was innocent. Buck knew without delay that it was a cover up for the rich kids. Someone else was to blame, but not his client. When the case went to court, Buck won. He was really happy because this is what he wanted to do. Clearing this young boy's life was a straight shot to success for Buck. He felt, more than ever, that this was his calling. To fight for the rights of all people. The first thing he did was call his dad

Ezra and told him about winning his case. Ezra was so happy. He knew his son was born to do some good in this world.

Ezra and Nova were enormously proud of Buck. They were getting up in age now. Ezra still worked at the fish factory and Nova was still working at the homeless shelter and doing housework for others. They were so proud of their children.

They were finally able to buy themselves a small home in New Orleans. Ezra still, in the back of his mind, wanted to build another home in the bayou. There was something about the bayou that made him feel free and more at home. It didn't have to be big or expensive. Just a place where he could go and visit occasionally. He had always made plans to do this, so one day he called some of his friends and told them he was ready to build his home. He would make it a house of brick and concrete. He would have to have to put it on stilts because of the hurricane season. To Ezra it was a place of peace. They finally started to build in the fall of the year when the leaves were falling off the trees. Ezra called Buck and Jennifer to come home for Thanksgiving. He wanted them to see what he had built. It was really modern.

The paint was beautiful. He put some of Jennifer's pictures on the walls and some of Nova's quilts over the couch in front of the fireplace.

Buck wanted to stay in San Francisco. He loved the beaches and the casinos. He would go for long walks along the beach. Just the smell of the ocean and the waves hitting the sand. He loved the mist from the ocean hitting him in the face. He would take his shoes off and go walking barefoot in the sand. Where he came from was not as nice as this. Buck would sit in his apartment, which was on a hill, and watch the sunrise and sunset daily. He thought to himself how beautiful it was. Most of the people from New Orleans loved the sun. They also loved being next to the body of water that surrounded the city. When he was growing up, he didn't pay much attention to it then. He grew to appreciate it when he grew older.

Buck was debating whether to come home for the holidays. He really missed his mom and dad. He was particularly close to his dad. They spent a lot of time together. His father taught him how to survive when tough times came. Buck saw a lot of challenging times, but he knew he had to make it on his own. He enjoyed being a lawyer. He loved helping people get their lives back. Buck was going to stay in San Francisco and help his clients. One day he wanted a wife and family but not right now.

Jennifer was doing quite well in Paris. She became rich very quickly. She loved modeling. By now, she had several modeling schools. She missed her mom and dad a lot.

She would call them about every other day when she had some spare time. She would tell them how things were going in Paris. She was always hoping things were going well at home.

One day Jennifer got some shocking news about her friend Madyson who lived in New York. She heard she had been killed. The authorities could not find the body and they could not find out who had killed her. Jennifer was heartbroken.
Someone told her she had overdosed. Jennifer knew that was a lie. Madyson never used drugs. She called her brother Buck the lawyer. She wanted him to go to New York to find out what happened to her. He was terribly busy and had to move some things around. Because it was his sister that he loved so much, he told her he would be in New York in a couple of days.

When he landed in New York he went straight to the police station to get the police reports and all the information he could get. The first thing he found out is that she was working a company that was a prostitution ring. She thought that it was a reputable company, but in reality, it was not. Madyson was very naive about things sometimes. They were using her photos for pornography, and she didn't know it. They were making lots of money off her pictures. One day she walked in on them talking about her photos and what they were doing with them. She became terribly angry and demanded they stop using her pictures in this way. That was when all hell broke loose for Madyson. She told them that she would not model for them anymore. Two days later they found her dead in a hotel room. The police said it was an overdose. That's where Buck came in. He had to prove them wrong. He traced her footsteps for the past 6 months to see what she was involved in. Everything seemed fine until her death. He then investigated everything that went on in her life for the last year. come to find out, she was working for the biggest cartel in the area. He said that they had murdered her. She didn't know who she was working for. The story goes that Buck brought them all to justice and put them all in prison for a long time. Jennifer loved him for that.

Jennifer and Buck's parents still wanted them to come for a visit. They both were able to finally get some time off work and they were able to visit at the same time. Their parents were really surprised. Ezra had built the new house where the old house had burnt down. It was really beautiful down in the bayou. There wasn't a house near them for a few miles. Ezra never wanted his family to forget the life that they lived in the bayou. They were glad to live where the moon and the stars shone bright at night. Everything else was always dark at dusk there.

This house was going to be a safe haven when they needed a place to get away from it all. Ezra and Amanda never wanted their children to think too highly of themselves. After all, Buck and Jennifer had both become very rich. They had a wonderful time staying with their parents for a few days, but they had to get back to work and live their lives.

Jennifer went back to Paris. Buck went back to San Francisco. It was bittersweet leaving their parents. They didn't know when they would be able to get away again to go see them. Ezra and Nova went to the airport with them to say their goodbyes.

Jennifer went back to Paris. She was getting tired of living all by herself. She had many men that wanted to date her but none of them mentioned marriage. She was so into her career in modeling that she had put her love life on hold. She realized one day that she had everything except love.

One afternoon she was walking through the zoo that was in the city. She loved animals. She was raised with them. She saw a cute baby tiger and she had something to give it. She was taught to never put her hands in front of their mouths unless you have something to give them. Suddenly, the baby tiger got a hold of her little finger and started biting it. A young man walking by grabbed her hand and pulled her loose. That was very scary for her. She lost half of her little finger. It was terrifying for her. How could she model with four and a half fingers? The young man was so sweet, kind, and handsome. When she looked into his eyes there was some type of tingle. It really turned her on to him. She got his name and phone number. It was a few weeks before she got the courage to call him. Jennifer asked him if she could take him out for lunch some time. He said yes. She took him to one of the best restaurants in Paris. During lunch she asked him what he did for a living. He said he was part owner of the zoo. At one time she was thinking of buying the zoo. She had to think twice about that now. She had thought about suing the zoo because of her accident. How could she sue someone who had saved her life. Right away she liked him and wanted to get to know more about him. They started dating. He had a yacht, and they went yachting several times. He always paid for everything. She knew he wasn't broke.

He had a motorcycle, and they went riding around the countryside frequently. They went together for one year. He wanted to marry him. Jennifer was ready to get married. He asked. She said yes. This was the first marriage for both of them.

They were married around Valentine's Day. It was a middle-sized wedding. Not too big or too small. Her parents couldn't attend because it was too far for them to travel. Jennifer sent them photographs of the wedding. They thought it was beautiful. Buck was able to attend. She was so happy about that. They were married two years and she became pregnant. She was incredibly happy, but her husband didn't seem very happy at all.

Jennifer delivered a baby girl. They called her Nomi. She looked just like the French people.

After the baby was born, she was worried about her figure. She had gained a few pounds due to her pregnancy. She also wondered if she could model again because of the baby and her little finger that was severed. She had excuses if she decided not to model again. She loved modeling but didn't know if she wanted to still pursue her career. She came up with the idea to open a modeling school for plus sized women. She knew there were plenty of larger women who wanted to model but were not given the opportunity to do so. Her school was highly successful and made a lot of money. Her clients were grateful to her. Some of them were featured in some of the biggest magazines in Paris.

Her husband didn't earn as much money as she did, but he was grateful for such a wonderful wife. One day Jennifer's accountant contacted her and told her that her husband was taking substantial amounts of money from her account. Jennifer questioned him and he said he had not taken any money without her knowledge. What her husband was doing was gambling. He was going to the casinos and horse races daily. He finally confessed that he had a gambling addiction. Jennifer was truly angry. She then found out that he was not part owner of the zoo. He was just a worker there that had been taking care of the animals when they met. He begged her for forgiveness. She lost a lot of trust in him and didn't know what to do. She loved him so much. She wondered if she could ever trust him again. He wasn't unfaithful to her, but he was a gambler. She asked him if he would get help for his addiction. He said he would. He got his addiction under control and Jennifer was happy again.

One day she was sitting on her porch and got a strange text. It was her friend Madyson. She didn't die that day in New York. She had to testify against the cartel. She had been put in witness protection living in Arizona. She was married and very happy. Through the years she wondered what really happened to her friend. Jennifer knew she could never see her again. She was so happy she was still alive. Madyson had her own modeling school in Arizona for kids. Madyson had three children. Two boys and one girl. She named her daughter Jennifer after her longtime friend.

In the meantime, her brother Buck was doing well in San Francisco. He had his own offices and had several lawyers collaborating with him. He was asked to assist in some high-profile cases. The Simpson and the bomber cases. He really loved what he was doing. He wanted to bring justice to all those people who were wronged. People who were wrongly accused of crimes they didn't commit. He finally got married and had five kids. He told Jennifer he was incredibly happy. He had a beautiful wife and a beautiful home.

Life was great and he never forgot where he came from. One morning he called his dad and said that he wanted to start a family reunion. He wanted all the family to come back to Louisiana. He wanted to have it in the bayou. Many relatives were living all over the world. It would have to be planned ahead of time so people could make travel plans. He told Ezra that they would make it the 3rd Sunday in July. It started in 1983 with Buck in charge. Plans were started and relatives contacted. It was a great reunion. They had raffles, dancing, and all kinds of activities for the children. Of course, there was plenty to eat. Not all of the people who attended were relatives. Some were friends that they had known for years. They decided that from now on, they would have the next reunion every one to two years. It would always be on the 3rd Sunday in July. Ezra said that the next time they came they would have a nice swimming pool so they could swim. Ezra asked Nova why they hadn't thought of having a reunion sooner. It was just like some of the festivals in New Orleans.

In the year 2005 was one of the worst hurricanes to hit New Orleans. It was really bad. Water came up over bridges, people were standing on rooftops waiting to be rescued. It destroyed a lot of low areas of New Orleans. To this day, there are people that were never able to return to their homes. Whole neighborhoods were wiped out. Most people were poor and had no insurance which didn't allow them to rebuild. One good thing for Nova and Ezra is that the hurricane did not touch their home in the bayou.

In San Francisco, Buck met a man from New Orleans who had gone through the hurricane. He was glad to meet someone from his hometown. They became great friends. He was an architect that built bridges. He told Buck how he had rebuilt some of the bridges in New Orleans after the hurricane. He had a genuinely nice family. Buck visited him often. He told him about the yearly reunion that they had started.

In the fall of the year, Ezra called Buck to see if he would be able to come to the annual alligator hunt. It lasted about a week. Buck thought to himself that he didn't know how he could, but he would figure it out. Buck knew this was the time of year that his dad made some extra money for the year. He said he would come and bring his friend Rico. They arrived in New Orleans and went directly to his parents' house in the bayou. Nova, his mother, was so happy to see him. She ran and threw her arms around him. It was a beautiful day when they got there. Buck liked it there because this is where his mom and dad lived. It was always peaceful and quiet there. Living in the big city, there was always some kind of noise. If it wasn't the trolley cars it was just the cars running up and down the streets and all the bright lights.

The next morning, Buck, Ezra, and Rico went down to the bait store and got their bait, lines and rented the boat to go alligator hunting. Buck paid for everything. They used chickens as bait. They got their trapping gear and whatever they needed. They had to take a rifle with them to kill the alligators once they were caught. Before they left, they heard there was a hurricane warning. As soon as they got out on the water, they could smell in the air that a hurricane was coming. They knew they had to hurry. This one seemed a bit different. They knew they had to step it up and get out of there. They sure didn't want to get caught up in the swamp with a storm coming. Rico had never been through anything like this before. The sky was getting darker and darker. The water was a muddy brown. Rico was a sharpshooter, so they gave him the rifle to shoot the alligators while they caught them. These alligators were huge. First, they caught them in a trap. Then they bring them up next to the boat. They shot them in the head and then brought them onto the boat. They shot them in the head so that the skin would be untouched which brought in more money. They shot one swimming down the swamp. They were allowed 8 to 10 alligators per season. The main reason for the hunts was to keep the alligator population down in the swamp and rivers. They used alligators for shoes, food, belts, and other accessories They could only hunt during designated seasons. Can you imagine putting a 400- or 500-pound alligator in a boat? It took at least two men or maybe more to accomplish the task. The gators really fought hard.

When they made it back to the bait store the manager asked them if they would help him get all the alligator hides out of the freezers and take them to higher ground. The hurricane was coming soon. First, they had to skin the gators that they had just caught so they could get their money. It was a hectic time. The manager wanted to make sure that all of the gators were safe in a freezer somewhere else. He could not let them spoil. They worked all day to get all of the gators into freezer trucks and taken away. Ezra made $20,000 that day. Thanks to Buck and Rico, Ezra made a lot of money that would last him through the winter months. All three enjoyed participating in alligator hunting that day.

There were companies that did boat tours in the swamps. They would bring them close to the alligators, snakes, and wild animals. It was a wild ride. They even had night tours. The tours would last 1 to 2 hours. They had men who carried rifles for the customers' protection against the wildlife, just in case. This was a very lucrative business.

It was finally time for Buck and Rico to leave Louisiana. Rico really enjoyed the trip. He told Buck that he would love to do it again. Buck, of course, was all for that.

Jennifer was doing very well. She had a modeling school for disabled children. She loved to watch them dance and grow. In Paris and nearby cities, it went well. Many of her students were featured in magazines. She instilled in the children that they could do anything if they tried hard enough. She taught them to never give up. The children loved it. They got to do things like other children, when sometimes they would be left out. Jennifer loved the smiles on their faces when she saw them modeling. Their parents were so grateful. One of her students was 16 and an excellent model. She was able to model at some of the greatest places. She was on TV a lot. She posted on Facebook. Someone saw her and wanted her to pose naked for them. She did what they asked. Before she knew it there were people asking her every day for nude photos. She wanted to stop but the man threatened her to say that he would hurt her if she stopped. She was so afraid. Jennifer noticed a difference in her, she was withdrawing herself increasingly. She had a talk with her and found out about what was happening. She broke down and started crying. She told Jennifer everything. Jennifer called the police and told her mother what was going on. The police came and said that this was happening a lot where they lived. A few weeks went by, and the police found the people who were doing this and put them in jail. They were glad that they were caught. After a few months the young lady started modeling again. This time she was ready and knew what to expect.

Ezra was still working at the fish factory and was taking the trolley home from work. His job was about one hour from home. This evening there were more people riding than usual. It was also more rowdy than usual. Suddenly two men got up out of their seats and started slapping and hitting people. Ezra never thought of this happening on the trolley cars here. They were two young punks. That's what Ezra called them. He was not going to stand for this. He jumped up and started to attack one of the men. The other robber was at the front of the trolley. Ezra almost got away with bringing the young robber down. The man at the front of the trolley started coming back toward him. He took Ezra down and almost knocked him out. But before he did, Ezra grabbed the man's mask and pulled it off. Ezra saw the man's face. He choked him until he passed out. They thought he was dead. They picked him up and threw him off the trolley. They threw him off on the worse part of the route. They made the driver stop and let them off. It was pitch dark where they threw him off. They thought he was dead and that no one would find him where they threw him off. Ezra came home at the same time every night and when he was late Nova began to worry. She called the trolley office, and they told her that there had been a robbery on that particular trolley. There were some injuries. She said that they had thrown Ezra off the trolley. They told Nova that they thought he was dead. In the meantime, Ezra woke up in the bayou in the dark and didn't know where he was. When he stood up, he could hardly barely walk. He checked to see if he had his cell phone. He tried to use it but there was no service. He knew that Nova would be worried. He knew he had to survive not only for himself but for Nova also. He wanted to put those punks in jail.

Ezra knew how to survive in the bayou. The first thing he did was grab a big tree limb and make a crutch for him. He was not afraid of trying to find something to eat. He knew every flower, berry, roots, and animals in the bayou. His father taught him how to survive out there years ago. He was a little worried about his physical condition.

By this time, Nova was worried to death about Ezra. She called all the family and told them what happened. Their friends said they would start looking for him around where they threw him off. They searched for 3 days. No Ezra. In the meantime, Ezra was moving toward the dense part of the bayou. He was in his sixties at this time. His heart wasn't that good, but he was not going to give up. There was water in some of the tree trunks that he used. He ate raw meat like turtles. He ate ants, and berries. He ate plants and flowers that weren't poisonous. It's amazing how you can survive in a place like this. It's just knowing how to do it.

It was the fourth day. He looked up and there were two young boys sitting near the swamp. Ezra yelled at them. They heard him and helped him to their house. Luckily, they had a cell phone. He called Nova and told her where he was. She was so happy that she nearly fell off her feet. She told him she and the squad would be after him right away. He was so lean. His color was terrible. He was dirty and very dehydrated. They took him right to the hospital. He would be fine in a day or two. Ezra knew one thing: he had to go back to his wife and family. He got better really quick. The police wanted to know who robbed him. He told them he saw one of their faces. I want to put them thugs behind bars for a while for hurting and robbing those people on the trolley. Right away he called his son Buck.

Buck came home immediately. He told his father that they would find the robbers. The police showed Ezra pictures of mug shots. He could not identify any of them. They checked his fingernails for any DNA of the robbers. There was no DNA evidence. For weeks they searched for them. One day Ezra was walking down at the food market in New Orleans. He was always looking around for the robbers. He was looking across the road and he got a glimpse of the robber who beat him up. He called the police, and they got him right away. Buck came right away to be with his dad in court. The court date was about two weeks after they found the man. The robber confessed and told on the other man who was with him. They both got twenty years in prison. Ezra and Buck were proud of themselves knowing that they were instrumental in solving the case.

Buck was recognized as one of the New Orleans folks in the paper. Buck work was done in the city for now.

Jennifer was still in Paris living it up. Do you remember the time she got half of her little finger taken off at the zoo? Well, she decided she wanted to have corrective surgery so she could have a full finger. She called a surgeon and started the process of getting a new finger. The doctor told her he would have to take her whole finger off and put a new one on. At first, she didn't like that idea so much. He told her she would have to be put on a donor waiting list. She really didn't like the idea of someone else's finger on her body. She waited four weeks before a donor finger was available. It was treated like any other transplant but not as serious.

Jennifer was still unbelievably beautiful. She was beginning to get some gray hair, but that was easy to fix. She could just use a little dye once in a while or wear a wig.

Jennifer told herself that now would be a suitable time to start designing clothes. She had thought about it for a while. She would design dresses, sweaters, and shoes. She found a building downtown that would accommodate them. She knew some exceptionally good seamstresses and put them to work.

She put ads in the local newspaper and magazines. She got lots of responses. She was so proud of the clothes that she designed. Her designs were influenced by her hometown of New Orleans. All the bright colors that were worn during Mardi Gras and other festivals in the city. Her clothes were worn all over Paris and the surrounding areas. Jennifer was extraordinarily successful in anything she put her mind to. She still had her modeling studio. She had so much money she didn't really know how much she was worth. One day she called her accountant to find out how much money she really had.

Her accountant Mike told her she was worth millions of dollars. She had an accountant she could trust. He told her if she never made another dime, she would have money for the rest of her life.

This is what I know. You can come from nowhere and still be successful in life.

One thing for sure she was always going to help anyone who needed her help. She sent her mom and dad thousands of dollars a month for additional income. She wanted to make sure they had everything they needed and more. She was so far away. She talked to them just about every day. They were getting up in age.

Getting back to what Buck was doing. He was working really hard on a lot of cases. One thing he took time for was to go to the beach and walk barefoot in the sand. He loved watching families enjoying themselves. He would go in the evening when he could watch the sunset over the ocean and watch the waves come in. He loved hearing the waves hit the shoreline. He still owned his boat and went yachting often.

Buck had a dream that one day he would go to see the pyramids. He was always thinking ahead of what he might do. Buck was a hardworking man and didn't really know how many people loved him. He was very honest and loving. He would tell you when something wasn't right. I guess that's why he wanted to be a lawyer in the first place. By this time, he and his family were pretty much settled. His kids were in school. His wife was a teacher for a high school in San Francisco. Her name was Amiyah and she and Buck had five children. There was always something for her to do at church and school. They both attended Calvary Missionary Baptist Church in San Francisco. It was an exceptionally large church that did a lot of good things for the community. The church had a food bank, clothing store, and a place for people on the streets and in parks. Amiyah and Buck wondered if the problem of homelessness would be solved.

They had a beautiful home and everything their heart desired. One day Buck said to Amiyah "Let's bring mom and dad out for a visit." Buck knew his parents were getting on in years and had never been out of Louisiana. He called them and they said yes, they would like to come, but not on a plane. They wanted to take a train. They were to leave on the 4th of July. It would take them 3 days to get there but it was worth it. They took pictures of the mountains and the small towns they went through. They saw a lot of Buffalo and deer along the way. They finally arrived in San Francisco. They were tired when they arrived but were so extremely glad to see Buck, Amiyah, and the kids. They went sightseeing. They rode on cable cars and went to Chinatown. They visited museums, the Golden Gate Bridge Park, and the California Academy of Science. They ate at nice restaurants and spent quality time with their grandchildren. Buck was so happy his parents were having an enjoyable time. They stayed for a week then it was time to take the train back to New Orleans. Buck really enjoyed their company even if it was only for a week.

He didn't know that this would be the last time he would see his father alive. Around Thanksgiving Buck got a call that Ezra had a heart attack and would have to have open heart surgery. So, Buck had to travel to New Orleans.

Ezra's health started to deteriorate. He had to go to a nursing home. Nova couldn't walk or hardly speak. This was a tough time for all of them. Ezra had dedicated his life to his family. Looking back on his life he was quite a man. I guess him growing up in the bayou made him strong. He was in the nursing home for about a year before he passed away.

Nova was all by herself living in the bayou. Buck wanted his mom to come and live with him in San Francisco. She told him that she would spend the rest of her life in the bayou where she had lived all her life. Nova was still in fairly good shape and could still take care of herself. Buck missed Ezra so much. He would definitely miss the gator hunts they went on. Ezra before he died said "Don't have a big funeral for me." He didn't want one of the funerals they had going down Bourbon Street. So, they had a small funeral at the church. Ezra always said he wanted to be buried someplace in the bayou. So that's what they did.

Buck went home after the funeral. He was walking the beach and a mother, and her two daughters were there looking for shells and feeling the ocean waves on their feet. They said hello and talked for a few minutes and exchanged names. One of the little girls' names was Marie. He told her that was a beautiful name. She said, "Thank you, Mister!" Her mom was a single mom who was working trying to make ends meet. He ran into them several times on his walks. Come to find out the little girl was making Tik Tok videos. She was so good that she got thousands of views and her videos went viral. Her mother's name was Alisa. She was hardworking but was barely making ends meet. Buck asked her what type of work she did. She said she worked in a restaurant. She had a high school education. Buck went home and spoke to his wife about hiring her as a receptionist. His wife said that it would be a clever idea to hire her. This is one of the many ways Buck helped people.

She worked for Buck's law firm for about a year and decided that she wanted to go to school to get a degree in something pertaining to the law. She knew so many of her race had been mistreated and beaten by the system. She even marched in the streets for civil rights. She wanted to rise up and help anyone she could in their situation. Even if she was a law clerk or working in the courtroom with the lawyers.

Alisa's daughter Marie, by this time, was 12 years old and very smart. She was a dancer. Her mother had started her dancing at the age of six. She was particularly good and won many trophies. She also made a small amount of money. She was a very smart young lady. She told her mother that she would like to work for the TV station and be an announcer or TV host. She told her mom that it would be a decent job and she would make a lot of money. Marie was always dreaming and would tell her mother and grandmother a lot of her dreams. She could see into the future with her dreams. Her mom, Alisa, told her to keep dreaming because sometimes dreams do come true. And that's just what Marie did. It's funny how when you are young you know what you are here for. She felt she knew where she was going and how to make it come true. Marie was gifted in other areas and could play the piano extremely well. When she was born, she had something wrong with her kidney. So far, she was doing well with that. One thing that Alisa always told Marie is that she could do anything she put her mind to. Marie would repeat this to herself often.

Well, getting back to the bayou, Jennifer and Buck's father, Ezra, had worked in the fish factory for years. His family got free fish from there during his employment. The plant processed turtles, crab, lobster, and alligator meat. For some reason after 65 plus years the plant was going to close. Jennifer and Buck heard about the closing and sent someone down there to figure out why it was shutting down. Come to find out the man running it was putting a lot of money in his own pocket. He was putting money in an offshore account. He was getting rich off the company and letting it go downhill. What a mess it was. Jennifer and Buck put a lot of money into the plant and got it started again. They knew that if the factory shut down it would make it hard on the people who worked there. They both always looked for a way to help other people. The accountant and the head of the company were put in jail. For a while.

Buck and Amiyah had five kids. One of the girls had decided she was going to Ohio State University in Columbus, Ohio. It was a big college. At first, they didn't want her to go so far away from home. They lived in San Francisco all her life, so she was used to the big city. Her name was Sophia. Sophia was very smart. She got straight A's her first year. She really liked the school and the professors. They knew she came from a very wealthy family. One day she walked into the parking garage to get her car. There were two men she never saw before walking up next to her. They wanted her car and her laptop. She wasn't going to give up her stuff that she had worked so hard for without a fight. She took her mace and sprayed it in their faces, but one of the punks got hold of her hair and pulled her down to the ground. She reached up and felt some blood running down her face. They stole her car, laptop, and some money. She called the police and then went to the hospital and got some stitches. Except for the stitches she was okay. She was really mad that they had stolen her car. She had worked hard for that car.

Sophia graduated college with honors. She was a veterinarian and went back to San Francisco and opened a veterinarian clinic. She had always loved animals and had an incredibly good business.

Sophia had met a young man in college and became extremely interested in him. She went with him for several months and finally they decided to get married. He was a high school teacher. His name was Hanford and things went well for them for a few years. They were drifting apart for some reason. Time went on and Sophia found out he was going with one of the high school students. He was fired and went to jail for a few years. So that ended Sophia's marriage.

The rest of Buck's children were doing well. By this time, they had six grandchildren.

Let's get back to Buck's sister Jennifer. As we know, she was a famous model in Paris worth a lot of money. She was always getting invited to all the social gatherings. She was always invited to the homeless charity activities, and she was always happy to go. The next charity event was going to be on Valentine's Day. Jennifer and her husband were always glad to be a part of anything concerning the homeless. It was almost 7:00 in the evening and they were getting ready to attend a charity event. Her husband said he wasn't feeling well, and she decided to attend the event by herself. It was just turning dark, and she got out of her car.
She noticed a strange looking car down the road from her

house. She didn't think much about it at the time. As she turned the corner and drove for a while down the road the car passed her going really fast. She was coming up on a railroad crossing. She saw that a train was coming down the track. She heard the whistle blow. She thought to herself that she was going to be late for the event. She had to stop. The train had also stopped the car that had passed her just a few seconds ago. Suddenly, they got out of the car, ran toward her car, opened her car door and pulled her out of it. She was screaming but no one heard her because of the train. Jennifer felt that she was going to be in for a lot of trouble.

One of the men had an accent. They took her to an old warehouse outside of town. It seemed as though she rode for two hours. She didn't know where she was. When they got there, they threw her onto the cold concrete. They gave her a bucket to relieve herself in. She was so cold that she thought she was going to freeze to death. When they arrived, there were four men there. Two sounded young and two sounded older. The older men were telling the younger men what to do. They took her phone from her. What they didn't know is that she had a tracer on her phone. She could be traced anywhere she went. When her husband couldn't get a hold of Jennifer, he called Buck. Buck was terribly upset. He told her husband that he would be there as soon as he could get there. Buck arrived in Paris at about 3:00 am. He and her husband

gathered their friends who knew the city. People who knew all the out of the way places. Places where it is easy to hide people. In the meantime, Jennifer was still on the floor of the warehouse. They did come in and feed her and give her water. While she was there, she had a lot of time to think of her life. How successful she was. She did not feel she had done anything wrong. The abductors were asking for 500,00 dollars for her release. She was worried about her family at home. She knew they would be worried about her. One of the young men brought her a blanket and a pillow. It made her feel a little more comfortable. Jennifer had heard about wealthy people being kidnapped but she never thought it would be her. She thought of her friend Madyson and what she had gone through. She thought what if they can't find her. She began to pray to God. She prayed to God that you know I am rich, and some people may want to take my life. Suddenly, a big light came through a crack in the window. She hoped it was a good sign, but she knew what was going to happen to her. Jennifer's mental condition was getting hard to handle. She never had to deal with this before. She remembered what happened to Ezra years ago. Thinking of him gave her a lot of inner help.
She knew she could get through this. She thought about the good times in her life and how she loved her father.

Luckily, the tracker that she had on her phone paid off. Her location began to show up on the computer. They called Buck and told him they had a hit on Jennifer's location. They finally located the warehouse. As soon as they got there the men started firing guns at them. The police finally were able to arrest them and put them into custody. Jennifer was bruised and cold, but she was all right. What a terrifying experience she went through. It was something she would never forget. She later found out that the men were part of a gang. They wanted the ransom money to help them get out of the country and get to Africa. Instead, they will be spending 20 years in prison. After Jennifer was rescued, Buck returned to San Francisco. Thank God for the tracking device. It saved her life.

Jennifer said it was time to take a trip and go back to the bayou. She didn't get to go very often because of how far it was, and she was always working. So, she and her family flew home. It was almost time for the Mardi Gras. Her children had never visited during this time of celebration. Jennifer decided while she was home, she would have a special party for the homeless children. She would put together a party really quick. She rented a big venue. She printed flyers and spread it by word of mouth. She decorated the place like never before. It was beautiful. She had a real band so they could do a lot of dancing. She wanted the party to be something they never would forget. She also gave out clothes, shoes, and personal items. There were close to 500 children. Jennifer was glad she was able to reach so many kids.

After the party she decided to take a trolley ride downtown. There was a chill in the air. As she neared the Hard Rock Cafe Hotel it started to collapse. The building was 190 feet high. It had a penthouse, 6 condominiums and apartments. People were screaming and telling the trolley driver to hurry and get out of the way. She escaped death again. They had been doing construction on the building on the lower levels. Some of the beams were not strong enough to hold the building. Mistakes were made in the construction. She hurried and got out of downtown. Bad luck seemed to follow her, but God was protecting her.

Nova was getting older and had been staying by herself since her husband died. Ezra had been her life. The years without Ezra were hard. Jennifer didn't know what they were going to do with her in the near future.

Buck and Jennifer wanted to take a trip somewhere warm. They said let's go to Hawaii. They knew this would take some planning. Jennifer and her family flew into San Francisco and met up with Buck and Amiyah. They decided to stay for two weeks.

Let's talk about Hawaii. The year Kamehameha was born he was a ruler. He was a ruler of the Hawaiian Islands national homeland in the Valley of Konoha. Konoha was one of the first born from a volcano more than 700,000 years ago. It has lots of mountains and deep valleys. The best way to see all the island was to fly over it in a helicopter. That's what the family did was take a helicopter ride, some of the cliffs were 1000 feet high. The island has many beautiful waterfalls, palm trees, and a lot of clear streams that you could drink straight from.

Buck and Jennifer wanted to visit all the Islands and all the cities. Their hotel was beautiful and had gold trimming and was a beautiful color of orange. One thing about the islands, there are beautiful colors everywhere. It is a paradise for visitors who can see things they have never seen before. There are gorgeous flowers, palm trees, and lots of sunshine. They got around by tour bus and shuttle buses. There was Uber and Lyft services, public transportation, and car rentals to get around in. They ended up renting a car so they could drive all over the island when they wanted to. By the way, the nickname for Honolulu is Paradise Island. Kauai is a pure paradise for people who love the outdoors. It is the oldest of all the major islands. It has beautiful flowers and the world's best beaches. Buck and Jennifer knew they had to get started to enjoy their vacation. They wanted to do a lot of shopping. There were shops all over the city. They could find and collect seashells. They could also visit many art galleries. There were many mountains and valleys on the islands. Jennifer was extremely interested in the native attire that the natives wore. She decided to purchase fabric and take it back to Paris when she returned to have some outfits made.

Buck loved the beaches and the clear blue ocean. He took many pictures of the beautiful scenery. There were all attractions for the children to do. There were water sparks, miniature golfing, bowling, and amusement parks. They all had a wonderful time. Finally, it was time to go home. Jennifer and Buck boarded different planes to return home.

Buck loved to travel and on the plane home he was already thinking about the adventure he wanted to embark on next year. He had always wanted to go see the Great Pyramids. Maybe that would be his next trip.

In the meantime, when he returned home, there was a case that he was concerned about. A young black football player who was in high school was put out because he was gay. He loved football and was exceptionally good at it. The young man was upset because he eventually wanted to play professional football. He knew if he couldn't play high school football it would severely diminish his chances for playing in the big leagues. The family called Buck. He took it to court right away. The judge was very fair. It took weeks for the verdict to come back. The jury decided that the boy was discriminated against and could again play on the football team. Although he won the case, he wouldn't be able to use the same locker room as the other players. To Buck, that was still discrimination, but he was happy he could play on the team. It was his last year to play anyway. He led his school to the championship and after high school was drafted to the Pittsburgh Steelers. He was a great linebacker and made lots of money. Later in life he was inducted into the Football Hall of Fame. Buck was incredibly happy for the young man and followed his progress through the years. When the young man's career was over, he would go and visit Buck. He was grateful for the help that he had given him as a young boy.

Though Buck's influence was fading as a lawyer, he still believed he could make a difference in the lives of many black people by helping them open their own business. He was getting older, but he didn't want to slow down. He wanted to continue to help people until he died.

Buck had three boys whose names were Kenny, Jimmy and Billy. Kenny was a strong young man growing up. He fought for whatever he thought was right. He graduated and went to college. After college he went to the Marines. Buck wasn't too happy about him enlisting. He served several years in Afghanistan and Buck worried about him the whole time he was over there. He was discharged and then reenlisted. Buck was immensely proud of him.

Jimmy was a little different. He was independent and carefree. He graduated from high school and decided he wanted to go to Florida. He went to Florida and lived on the beach. He was like his dad. He loved the ocean. He could also do almost anything that pertained to the inside of a home. He was particularly good at what he did. He would visit San Francisco from time to time but he made Florida his home.

Billy was also in the armed services. He was in the Army. He served in several countries and made it his career. He served in many tours of duties and ended up with Agent Orange. It affected him in many ways. Buck was so proud of all his boys.

Buck had a daughter named Karla. From a small child she wanted to be an activist and an entertainer. She loved to play the piano and had a lovely voice. She was a restless child and Buck knew that restlessness would take her to various places. She went to Las Vegas and worked there for many years singing and dancing at the casinos and hotels. She made a good living and was able to take care of herself. Buck was proud of her, but she never told him what kind of life she was really living. She got mixed up with a sex slave ring. There were always men who wanted something different than what their wives would do for them. Karla had a very level head on her shoulders. She knew when to stop doing things. Karla was the only kid that Buck worried about. He didn't know one day from another what she was doing. One day he got a call from one of her friends saying that she hadn't heard from her in a while. She sounded as though she was really upset. Buck thought that was strange because he hadn't heard from her either. She always called on Sunday. Karla had mentioned that she thought someone was stalking her. Some of her clients were really nuts about her. This had happened before for her, but she always got it straightened out. This fellow was rich and had a wife and family who lived in Las Vegas. He would pay her $1000 every time she performed for him. All she had to do was tie him up and spank him and put a blindfold over his eyes. This is one of the many things she did for her customers. One night he asked her if she would spend a weekend with him. She started to say no but he offered her $2000, so she decided to go. It was supposed to be a beautiful weekend. He had a cabin in the mountains. She wanted to know where they were going. Before she left, she checked to make sure the place was legit. They started out, so far so good. They kept going farther and farther up the hill. He finally stopped and there was the cabin. She said okay. Little did she know that she was in for a rude awakening. It was really a wonderful place. She brought all the rough stuff that she knew he liked. She was going to make this a really good night for him. She brought a whip, some eye masks, and whipped cream. He seemed to enjoy it. After she was done with him, he grabbed her and put her down on the bed and tied her up. He said he was going to give her some of the stuff she had been giving him. She thought to herself "I've got a meathead." She was taught how to handle clients like this.

She was exceedingly small and only weighed about 120 pounds. She knew that she would have to go along with it for right now.

She didn't know she would have to be like this for quite some time. They were gone for two weeks in the cabin. As long as he didn't hurt her, she would continually put on the show for him. After 2 weeks she told him I must go home. He didn't want to hear that. He had fallen in love with her. Now, this was a problem. He told her he would never let her go. She knew by now that people would be missing her. Including her family. He still wouldn't listen. He took her cell phone. She was really in a mess. She may never be found for months. She was losing weight being all tied up. Whenever he left, he would keep her all tied up. He told her he loved her. That's why he was doing all this stuff to her. Every once in a while, he would talk about his life as a child. He talked about how his father would beat him. His mother would sit by and let him do it. He really had a mixed-up mind. He thought that's what you do to people you love. Karla asked him when she could go home. He told her when his money ran out. She guessed he was a millionaire so that didn't tell her a thing.

Meanwhile, Buck and the police were looking for her. It was cold in the mountains with not much sunlight. Karla tried and tried to get loose, but she was tied up with chains. One day he said he was going to the store for some food and other things that were needed. Some hand soap and lotion were accidentally left next to the bed. The chains around her wrists were just loose enough that there was some space between her hands and the chains. She was chained to the bed. She tried to get the chains off using the lotion. He didn't return until nighttime, but she still couldn't get the chains off. He returned and the next day he had to leave again. He told her he would be gone for a few days. Karla thought that this may be her way of getting out of there. She convinced him to take the chains off her legs because she had to use the restroom. He said okay. She told herself that this was her chance to get out of there. She knew it would be a struggle to leave the cabin, going down the mountains by herself, but she sure was going to try. She saw a small saw when she went to the bathroom. She sawed the chains off her hands. It felt good to be free of those chains. She was kind of weak and wasn't sure of her way down the mountain side. She heard that there were bears, coyotes, snakes, and all kinds of animals waiting to devour her. Whatever the risks she knew she had to take the risk and get out of there. She remembered what her grandpa Ezra told her if she ever got into this type of situation. He told her what she could eat and drink. She put on three pairs of pants and three sweaters. She found some boots and a coat. She was ready to go. She found some matches. There were some snowshoes in case she ran into a lot of snow. She got out of the cabin. Lo and behold she heard a car coming up the road. She knew it had to be her abductor. It was just getting dark. She ran into the woods. She could see him looking around for her. He finally left to look for her. Karla knew she was facing a tough situation. The cabin was by itself in the mountains. No one ever came near it. She never heard any cars or anything when she was there. She knew her dad, Buck, would be worried sick about her.

She knew they would be trying to find her by now. She knew she would have to stay off the road. She wished she could find a cabin with someone living there. It was almost dark. In some places there was snow up to her knees. She wanted to get as far away from there as she could. And especially him. She was so glad that her grandpa Ezra showed her a few things about living in the wilds. Some women would have given up, but not Karla. She had her father Buck's strength and will power. That's one thing about him that rubbed off on her. She was not about to go down without a fight. She stumbled through the mountains all night. She thought that she couldn't be far from Las Vegas. There must be someone who comes up this mountain once in a while. It was about 4 o'clock in the morning. She thought she saw a light in the distance. It looked like it was a filling station. And it was. The only thing about it was that there was nobody there at the time. She saw an outhouse in the back of the station. She went out there and stayed until she heard someone coming to the station to open it up. She got out of the outhouse and went to the door. When the man saw her at the door, he was startled at first. He finally let her in. She explained to him what had happened to her and wanted to know if she could use his phone. She called her dad. It was about two hours before he got to her. The man at the station gave her something to eat and drink. He gave her a blanket to warm up.

When Karla was reunited with her dad it was one of the best family reunions ever. Buck told her family that they found her, she was okay, and that she was coming home. They were so relieved. Karla went back home with her dad to San Francisco and stayed there for a while. All was well again. They never caught the man who kidnapped her. Some say he left the country and went abroad.

In the fall of the year, Jennifer and Buck got a call concerning their mother, Nova. She had been hospitalized with a new virus called Covid-19. She was up in age and rather frail. They both rushed to her side in the hospital. The doctor said that it was just a matter of time for her. It was a very sorrowful time. When she died it just didn't seem real. They had their mother with them for so many years. They thought how they would ever get along without her. It was just like a dream or some kind of fog when she died. Their hearts were broken knowing that she would be gone. Buck said it was her time to go. That's one thing that we all must do at one time in our life. Nova lived to be 89 years old. Jennifer said that living in the bayou was a quiet place for her. She was buried next to Ezra.

By this time, Buck and Jennifer were up in age. After living in San Francisco for so many years, Buck was getting tired of the hustle and bustle of the big city. His eyesight was getting bad. His children were all grown up and gone. He had lots of grandchildren. About 32 of them. He was a happy man and did what he wanted to do all his life. He had helped so many people. He got lots of people out of jail who were wrongfully convicted. So, he and Amiyah decided to move back to the bayou. It would be so quiet there with no pressure on them. The house was just like his dad left it. Ezra had fixed it up. He had remodeled it. It was just like a new house. There were a lot of memories there, Some good and some bad. Buck decided that he wouldn't set up an office in New Orleans, but if someone needed his help, he would help them out.

Every year, in the bayou, was alligator hunting season. Sometimes he would go down to the bait store and talk to the owner. It really was a good business, at least two seasons a year. They would talk about all the good times they had when Ezra was around. Every now and then some of the friends that went alligator hunting with would come by and catch some alligators together. They loved the sport and the comradery. The bait store owner was named Happy. Why they gave him a name like that Buck would never know.

Buck and Amiyah lived through several hurricanes but were not really affected by them. Buck equipped his home with a battery-operated radio. They had fireplaces for heat. They purchased a large generator to provide lights. They even volunteered to go out and help with rescuing people. They even opened their home during these times to people who were left homeless by the hurricanes.

Jennifer was doing very well in Paris. She loved it there. At times, she also longed to be back in the bayou. Her children were all grown up. She had 10 grandchildren. She was living like a queen. She had a beautiful home with two swimming pools and lush flower gardens. She was living high on the hog, as some people would say. Everyone she knew loved her. She had a glorious smile and a sweet personality. Even when she was young, she stood out amongst her friends. She always told her mother, Nova, that she would be a queen someday. She was always dancing and wearing fancy clothes. Nova had always bought the best of everything. Most of the time, Nova made her clothes.

While living in Paris, Jennifer did a lot of good things. She opened a dancing and modeling school for handicapped children. She built a homeless shelter and helped the local hospital and other charities. She was well known in Paris. Over the years she really missed her mother. She did get to go back home before she passed away. She owed all her strength and courage to her mother. She regretted that she didn't have more time with her parents while they lived. But that's neither here nor there. One thing about her parents was that they were enormously proud of their daughter. She had an Aunt Jo when she was young. Sometimes she would talk about her problems if she had any.

After Ezra and Nova died there had not been a reunion of the family for a while. Since Buck lived in New Orleans, he thought they should have a really big reunion at the park where they originally had them years ago. It was a small park in a place called Pennsville. All the relatives from both sides wanted to come. They put tents and extra tables all over the grounds. It was a beautiful site to see. They had a live band so everyone could sing and dance. Everyone was happy to see each other again. The reunion was the high point of the summer. Someone would always make homemade ice cream and give it to the kids. There were lots of pictures taken. After all, wasn't that what reunions were for?

As Jennifer and Buck grew older, they weren't as active as they used to be. Jennifer was still a classy lady. Her hair and makeup had to be exactly right. She was burned out from modeling and certain things about it. After all she made lots of money and was quite comfortable with her life. She could sit on her porch, in her swing, and watch the sunrise in the morning and the sunset in the evening. Yes, she was very satisfied with her life. She had done a lot of good in her life.

Buck was a little different. He loved to travel. He, like his sister, had done a lot of good things for people. He was happy with his life. He was content, and he wasn't looking for the unexpected. When he was 83 years old, he found out that he had liver cancer. That threw him for a loop.

He never thought he would have anything like this in his life. Even though he knew cancer ran in his family. He went to the best doctor he could find. The treatment lasted a while. He had a treatment called I90 for the liver. Two months later he developed cancer in the throat. He took treatments for that. He really hated that treatment. In the end, he developed blood cancer. He was tired of taking all of those treatments. So, on December 6, 2022, he had to let it go. He knew he couldn't beat this one. He knew it was time for him to die. He was so brave. All his children and some of his grandchildren were there. He gave up his life to God with his family holding his hands. It was so strange that morning. It's as if he knew that would be his last day on earth. He didn't get out of bed. He had a bad Saturday and Sunday night. Amiyah wanted to call the ambulance both nights, but he said no. On Monday morning Amiyah called the doctor and he said there is nothing more they could do for him. A little after noon he gave up the ghost and left this world. This broke everyone's heart. Amiyah knew it was his time. The family loved him so much. He had done so much for them. Amiyah wondered how she would live without him. There was a big funeral in the streets of New Orleans. There were a band and people following the hearse. He loved the song "Your grace and Mercy". He was buried next to his father in the bayou not far from where he lived. I don't think that when he was living that he knew how many people cared about him. He didn't know how much he was loved.

Jennifer lived ten years after he died. Before she died, she was dreaming of dancing in Paris with all the famous people she knew. She was driving home one night, and it was pouring. It was also very foggy. She had an accident, and it took her life. The family had a beautiful funeral for her. Famous people from all over the world came to pay their respects. She, like her brother, was buried in New Orleans. It was one of the biggest funerals also. She was dressed like a queen. Even though she was 80 years old she looked like she was 50. She was buried in the bayou alongside Ezra, Nova, and Buck.

This is my story about two people who lived their lives to the fullest. Both were loved and will be cherished for the rest of the family's lives. Both are gone but never forgotten.

With Love,

Written by,

Jo Ellen Tabler Scott Mayle

May 3, 2022

I would like to thank all my children.

    Brenda Payne

    Dorothy Wyatt

    Donald Mayle

    Michael Mayle

    Amy Payton

Thanks for putting up with me all these years. Love you all.
~~~~Mom

Made in the USA
Columbia, SC
27 November 2022